MARSHMALLOW
& JORDAN

MARSHMALLOW
& JORDAN

ALINA CHAU

:01
First Second
NEW YORK

HEY! Watch it!

Sorry!

One more lap, everyone!

BAM!!

First week of the fall semester

OKAY! Let's wrap up with a handoff shooting drill.

Gather yourself

Shoot

Get that elbow in

Aim

10

I'm going to tell Mom you're bullying me!

Jordan?

I'm okay. It's just...

...sometimes I wish I could play again.

J, I am SO proud of you. Look how much you've accomplished!

Coach would never have let a little kid sub for him—until you!

You're a b-ball whiz!

15

whimper

Who's crying?

HALO?

18

OH MY!

Are you alone?

Where did you come from?

It's okay...

19

You're welcome.

I made a new friend today!!

And it's an elephant!

Oh...my!

It's a white...elephant.

Nenek, can you take a look at his left leg? He's injured.

Wait a moment... I have something that will make you feel better.

I'm home.

Hi, Mom!

AHHHHH!!!

40

Do not worry so much.

It's eating the offering flowers too?

Ma...an elephant is not supposed to eat meat. It'll get sick.

It's okay.

Mom...can you take a look at the elephant? His leg is injured.

47

Mom, how bad is his wound?

It's pretty deep.

Can you fix him?

The antibiotic will help.

Will he be okay?

Yes. We just need to make sure the wound doesn't get infected.

49

Lord Ganesh,
please watch over the elephant.
Please help him heal.

How are you feeling?

I brought you dinner.

Eat up!

OH! AH-HA!! You like Marshmallow!

Marshmallow! Stop trying to steal my food!!

Let's check whether there's a missing elephant before we decide.

The child prayed to Lord Ganesh for the elephant. I overheard her.

Onde Dikit never asks the gods for anything for herself. What if Ganesh answered her prayer? Marshmallow stays!

RING!!

Good morning, class.

Good morning, Mr. Al-Samarrai.

Open your book to page thirty-two. Today we are going to explore the Pacific Ring of Fire. The geography of Indonesia is dominated by volcanoes that are formed due to movement within the subduction zones between several tectonic plates, including the Eurasian and the Indo-Australian...

...About 90% of the world's earthquakes and 81% of the world's largest earthquakes occur along the Ring of Fire...

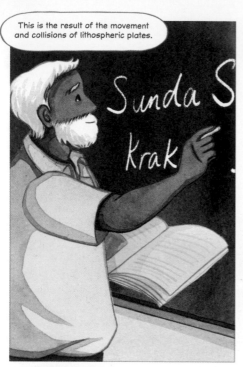

This is the result of the movement and collisions of lithospheric plates.

Pssst!

68

What's going on?
U never late to class. -L

JORDAN! What are the two most active volcanoes on Java?

Krakata

Errrr...

Kelud and Merapi.

It's Halmahera... and uh...

71

77

I heard the big news! Congrats, girl!

Huh? What for?

Paul has had a thing for you since forever. So happy for you two! It's about time!

Kris! Not you too...

Come on! Seriously, it's an elephant, not a boy.

J, if Paul ever makes you cry for any reason, we've got your back!

Oh good, you're here, Jordan!

Marshmallow?! Nenek?

Sooo soft...

Nenek, is everything okay at home?

Marshmallow has been whining since you left for school, so I brought him with me to pick you up.

He is very attached to you, Onde Dikit.

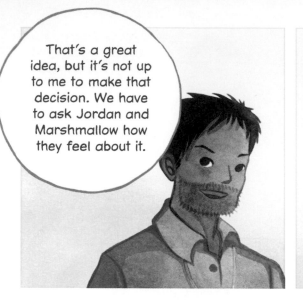

That's a great idea, but it's not up to me to make that decision. We have to ask Jordan and Marshmallow how they feel about it.

That would be awesome! I'm sure Marshmallow would love to join the team!

Welcome to the team, Marshmallow!!

YAY!!

YAY!!

YAY!!

Let's start with this poster of Michael Jordan. He's a LEGEND!

He's retired now. He's older than Dad, but not as old as Nenek.

He was awesome, and he was Dad's favorite.

That's why he named me Jordan.

Steph's speed and consistency, combined with his incredible quick release, give him the advantage...

...during that split second before his opponents can close him out.

A second can make all the difference! I learned how to shoot from studying his moves.

I dreamed I'd be like him when I grew up... But that was before the accident.

So cute!
She's teaching
Marshmallow how to
play basketball.

A few weeks later

Lynn!

Team Lynn finally scores one point!

GO, MARSHMALLOW, GO!

PASS THE BALL TO JORDAN!!

Time's up! Final score: two to one. Team Marshmallow wins! Yay!!

That was an awesome game!

You rock, Marshmallow!

You're one very talented elephant. I wish my sister were half as good as you!

Hey, Hans! I heard that!

You aren't jealous of a baby elephant, are you?

Aren't you supposed to support me?

Okay... You did well!

But, what can I say, Team Marshmallow is just much much cooler!

What kind of brother ARE you?

Loser pays for ice cream!

Jordan is so good.

At this rate, I'll be broke from buying you ice cream!

Too bad she can't join us at Regionals. It's so unfair! Just because she's in a wheelchair.

That's the official rule, and we all know it. Even Jordan.

Yeah...

It's been two years... She understands why she can only play with us at practice.

Still, it's hard to see her look so sad when we assign the team roster each year.

Marshmallow! Let's go!

We're going to Anita's for ice cream! Lynn is TREATING us!

She said it's ALL-YOU-CAN-EAT pineapple Cold Whip today!

WHAT?! I didn't say that!

Listen, you two, just one Cold Whip per person!

WOW...

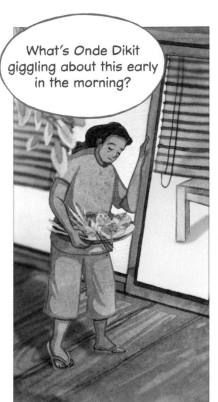

What's Onde Dikit giggling about this early in the morning?

SPLASH SPLASH

This is easier than expected!

Ma?

Look!

It's wonderful to see her swimming. It's been so long.

131

Meanwhile, at home

Now let's go get some mango and durian.

Why are we getting so much food?

It's for Nenek's sewing club meetup at the temple.

I thought there were only four or five old ladies in her sewing club. That's a lot of food for just them!

Never under-estimate the superpowers of little old ladies.

Haven't you seen those eating contests on TV? Most of the time the winners are scrawny!

I'm always curious where they put all that food?

Dad, are you implying Nenek and her friends eat like pigs?

Is there anything we can help with?

Jordan'll be back soon. If you can help set the rest of the table, that would be great!

Coach, Taman. Thank you for coming. Oh, little Buana has grown so much.

138

WHAT?!

They've got a point! Otherwise, we'll just hang around the hoop.

FWEET

ROUND TWO!

Coach is the referee. You can't boss us around!

Terima kasih!

Yeah, right! He's not even watching the game.

Round Two! Ready? Go!

PENALTY!

Alyssa! THE BALL!

Oops...

GO, JORDAN, GO!

BLOCK HER!

Don't let her pass the ball to Lynn!

She should see about joining the school water polo team. I bet with training she could compete.

Compete...with the school water polo team, huh?

Jordan scores again! Two to zero!

What? How?

DANG! She just swished that from more than half the length of the pool! She can channel Steph Curry in the water too?

WOW! It's a Marshmallow team jersey!

Marshmallow, thank you.

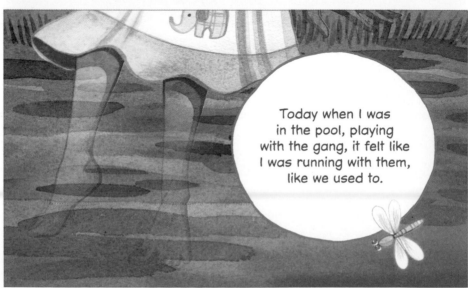

Today when I was in the pool, playing with the gang, it felt like I was running with them, like we used to.

Shirin, this is Jordan. The student I told you about.

Jordan, very nice to finally meet you. Coach Prayogo raves about you.

Have you played water polo before?

No, but I can't wait to learn the game.

Great! Let me introduce you to the team.

FWEET

Er...yeah, I'm on the basketball team.

Since Amisha graduated last spring, we haven't been able to find anyone good enough to recruit for competition.

Jordan comes highly recommended by Coach Prayogo. She'll be a perfect fit for our team.

Is she gonna be able to compete?

What?

Can she even swim?

Let's take a break while Jordan is getting ready.

It may take some time for the kids to warm up to Jordan.

Does she know this is a leg sport?

It's unfortunate that in a small town like ours, there aren't any disabled leagues. This will give Jordan a chance to be an active athlete in a school team.

Let's have you start with a few laps, so we can analyze how to tailor your training to your strengths.

Meanwhile...

Today we're going to start prepping for Regionals.

Lynn, you'll be the new team captain.

What about Jordan?

Some of you already know that, unfortunately, official rules won't let Jordan compete at Regionals.

She's still part of the team, right?

Jordan IS on the team and she can come to the games with us, but she can't compete.

Then why isn't she here today?

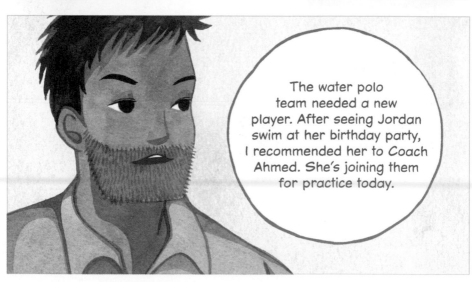

The water polo team needed a new player. After seeing Jordan swim at her birthday party, I recommended her to Coach Ahmed. She's joining them for practice today.

You've got great upper-body strength! However, you'll need to learn how to use your upper-body muscles differently to build more speed.

Hey, Wayan!

Huh?

This means war!

HEY, you two!
The competition is right
around the corner.

Can you TRY to take practice seriously?!

With a sea slug joining the team, our chances of passing the first round are slim as it is.

URGH!

Let's wrap it up!

Coach, can I stay and practice a little longer?

Of course you can. Just don't overdo it.

Mom just texted again. Ojichan is getting cranky.

Make sure J gets home safe.

Halo, Jordan.

Halo...

Can I see your drawing?

Sure, but the drawings are still very rough.

WOW! These are amazing!

You're very good!

Thanks!

By the way, I don't know your name.

I'm Paola.

You'll love this manga! It's funny.

Hey, J!

Hey, everyone!

We've been looking everywhere for you!

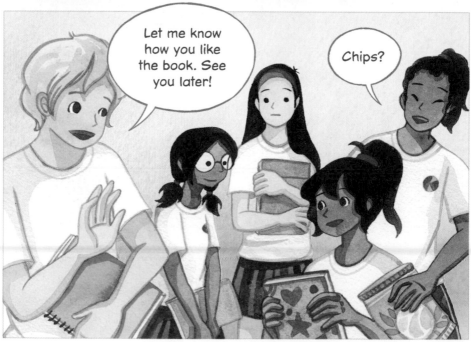

Let me know how you like the book. See you later!

Chips?

And your first game as captain. I wouldn't miss it!

Promise?

Pinky promise!

You know, this will be our very first game in middle school too!

You're well prepared. Don't worry about the score. Just do your best and have fun out there!

GO, Kahawaii, GO!

FWEET

WHY?

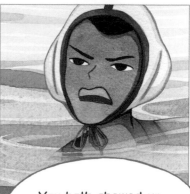

You both showed up late and you were goofing around half the time.

Not fair! Our class ran late!

TWENTY LAPS! The sooner you finish, the sooner you can go.

Jordan, I'll work with you on some offensive and defensive tactics.

Stroke.

Chop cross.

This technique allows you to fence off your defender to free yourself.

Now you try.

Pretend I'm your opponent. GO!

Not bad.
Let's go through it a few
more times.

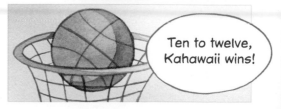

Ten to twelve, Kahawaii wins!

Still at the pool

Paola...

Jordan, what happened? How come you're all wet?

Kemala made me stay for extra practice. I rushed here as soon as I could...

Let's get you dried off!

Look! We're in the school paper!

Halo, everyone!

Congrats...

Kemala!

Kemala, what's bothering you?

I'm afraid I'll be disqualified for the sports scholarship.

Our farm isn't doing well because of the drought. I need the scholarship to pay for tuition.

You get good grades. I'm sure you'll be okay.

NO! I won't be okay if we lose in the first round.

?

We're missing a player, and not everyone takes practice seriously.

But we're NOT missing a player.

COME ON, Sarah! Jordan is useless! She barely swims.

She's okay. She's actually getting better.

OKAY IS NOT GOOD ENOUGH! The game is next month.

Three weeks until the game

Marshmallow, what's up?

Where did you come from? You are LATE!

Have you talked to J lately?

NO!

I don't know what happened between you two, but you should check in with her sometime.

241

Lynn?

Hey, J...

Are you here alone? Where's your team?

They're done with practice already.

Why are you still here, then?

I need to do extra work to prepare for the competition. I don't want to drag the team down.

Why do you think you'll drag them down?

Cuz I can't swim fast enough, and I still have so much to learn.

I'm sorry.

I missed your first game. I had to stay behind for extra practice that day.

Hey, J!

Alyssa! Dea! What're you doing here?

Lynn called us to help you out. She's taking Marshmallow to the game.

What?! How?

Don't know... She was kinda mysterious about it.

256

259

AWWW... What should I do???

Isn't there a cap hanging on the locker door?

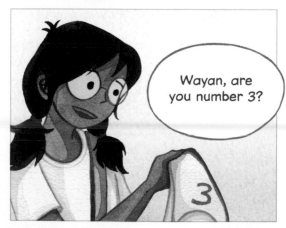

Wayan, are you number 3?

YAY! That's mine!

It's time!

Why am I nervous. I'm not even playing!

I know, right?

GO, KAHAWAII, GO!

OMG, is that a baby elephant?

Here is your stop. I'll be cheering for you!

Good luck!

Terima kasih, everyone.

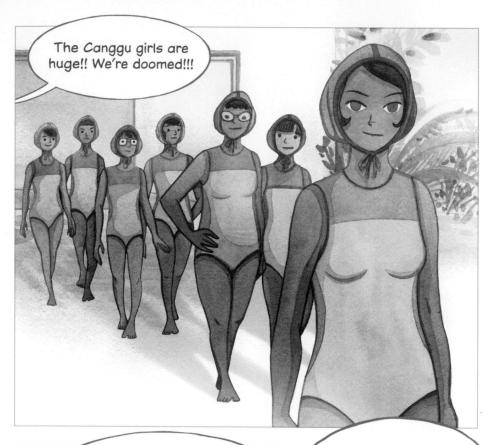

The Canggu girls are huge!! We're doomed!!!

Are they even middle schoolers? They look like high school kids.

That's because most of them are fourteen. Their captain, Lestair, is the highest-ranked swimmer in our district.

Lestair is FAST! Kemala can't even get close enough to block her.

Ndari, catch!

JORDAN!

OH NO!

This is not a good start...

I'm blocked!

Sarah's stuck...

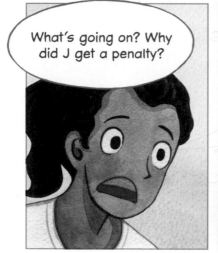

What's going on? Why did J get a penalty?

She gets a twenty-second penalty for pushing that girl underwater.

Don't get down on yourself. This is your first game. Mistakes happen.

That girl's totally faking it! How could J push her down? She's so much bigger than J.

Oh NO! Canggu scores again...

Jordan, you can go back now. Good luck!

GO, Jordan, GO!

Amanda, catch!

GO, KAHAWAII, GO!

Second period begins!

PAOLA! Give the ball to Amanda!

How come she won't pass the ball to J?

J is totally open. There are no defenders near her.

Sarah!

I think they're worried, after her earlier mistake.

She needs a chance, though.

YAY! Now we're even!

Finally, I can relax a bit.

Wayan, WATCH OUT!

Amanda, catch!

286

KEMALA, PASS THE BALL TO JORDAN!

KEMALA! PASS THE BALL TO JORDAN!!!!

Time's running out! Give the ball to Jordan!

TRUST US! JORDAN CAN SCORE IN TEN SECONDS!!!

There's no way your team can score in ten seconds.

WHAT?!

NO WAY!

YES!

Three Seconds

Two Seconds

SCORE!

YAY!! WE WON!

That shot was unbelievable for a middle schooler.

She is especially gifted.

...

She scored from the twenty-meter line. How's that possible?!

That was so awesome!

Terima kasih, Sarah.

You should have seen the looks on the other team's faces when you scored!

Jordan.

Glad to have you on the team.

Kemala...

Terima kasih.

Kahawaii vs.
Bangung School

Kahawaii vs.
Surabaya International

Kahawaii vs.
Diakonia Public
School

Kahawaii vs.
Tangerang Academy

Kahawaii vs.
Pelangi School

District Champions
Kahawaii Water Polo Team

Kahawaii is one of the strongest contenders for the National Finals. The team is led by Kemala Nalapraya...

She is a familiar face to fans of middle school water polo.

Hey, girls!

LOOK! We're FEATURED on *Lesser Sunda Aquatic* vlog!

That's HUGE!

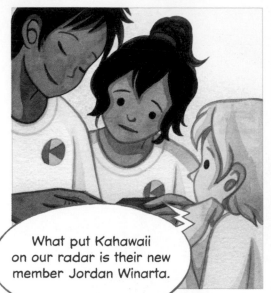

What put Kahawaii on our radar is their new member Jordan Winarta.

Her precision in long-distance shooting makes her the second-highest individual scorer in this season's tournament.

J, you're famous!

Now that Jordan is in the spotlight, she'll be under a lot of pressure.

The highest-scoring player is still Kemala Nalapraya...

Kemala! That's a NICE shot of you!

Regional Finals will be very competitive.

You worry too much. With you and Jordan on the team, we're UNBEATABLE!!

LISTEN!

With the two highest-ranking players on the same team, we predict that Kahawaii will advance to Nationals.

We need to defeat Bali Academy to qualify. Don't forget they won the national title last year.

Kemala has a point.

Both Jordan and Kemala will be heavily defended in the upcoming competition.

It'll be a lot harder for them to score.

Haven't you noticed that Kemala's scoring rate dropped in the last couple competitions?

Yup!

You'll need a new strategy. I've been analyzing all your competitions. Here's a plan.

J, you need to improve your short-distance acceleration speed to break away from the opponent's defense.

That should give you the crucial extra second to get the ball.

Kemala, when you're trapped inside five meters...

...It's okay to let your opponent get the ball.

WHAT?!

Wayan, you're great at defense. You'll be responsible for stealing the ball back.

Pass the ball to another teammate.

Whoever catches the ball can pass it back to Kemala.

Kemala, you'll be J's decoy. As soon as you've got the ball, the opponents'll block you.

This will weaken their defense on Jordan.

Now you'll pass the ball to Jordan.

J, you may still have at least one person blocking you.

You need to push your speed to the limit to catch the ball...

...and shoot!

That's a very risky plan.

It's wild, but it should get you out of some sticky situations.

Kahawaii wins!

Lesser Sunda Regional
Middle School Water Polo Champions

Congratulations, everyone. I am very proud of you.

Jordan!

Marshmallow is here. Let's go!

Coming!

Is everyone going to Anita's later?

Yup.

I'm not going to miss out on FREE TOPPING DAY!

Marshmallow will be meeting us at the gate.

Let's meet after assembly.

As our academic year draws to a close, we have much to celebrate.

First, I would like to congratulate Kahawaii Middle School Water Polo team for winning the Regional Finals.

Our middle school basketball team also had a successful year.

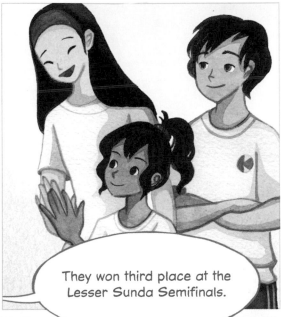

They won third place at the Lesser Sunda Semifinals.

While we have much to celebrate, we must not forget we are currently living through the most severe drought in the history of our island.

Many of our friends in the agricultural community are suffering from devastating financial losses due to the drought.

In order to reduce water usage at Kahawaii, the school will be shutting down all aquatic facilities this summer and the following school year, unless the situation improves.

The Kahawaii School Board and the Parents Association have set up a donation site...

...to help raise funds to support students and families in need during this climate crisis.

I would like to wish you all a restful summer vacation and I look forward to welcoming you back next academic year.

Dea, you're quiet today. Are you all right?

I was going to tell you guys later. I'll be transferring to another school next year.

Why? Not you too.

My dad got laid off from the farm last month. He's looking for a new job on other islands.

Didn't your dad work at Batukaru? They're one of the biggest farms.

Let's go to Anita's. We should still celebrate the end of the school year.

I'm going to miss everyone.

It has been a fun year.

Where is Marshmallow?

He was here a moment ago.

Maybe he went to the pool? Or the basketball court?

Don't worry, J. We'll spread out and find Marshmallow. You stay here, in *case* he *comes* back.

Marshmallow?

I'm going to check the classroom. You go check the lunchroom.

Okay!

Marshmallow?

Marshmallow?

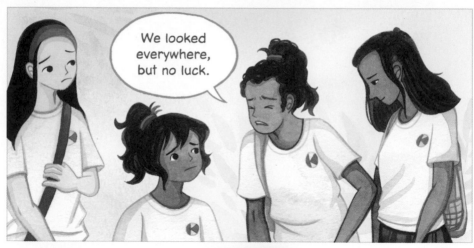

We looked everywhere, but no luck.

We looked all over the campus. We can't find him either.

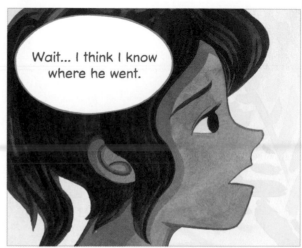

Wait... I think I know where he went.

I'm the cause of the drought.

The drought is no one's fault. Nobody can control the weather.

I'm your regional rain cloud. Since I came here, there hasn't been any rain.

I don't understand...

I live in the sky. The day you found me was the day I ran away from home. I tripped and fell to Earth.

Back home, I didn't really have any friends. Everyone made fun of me...

...and teased me, and called me "crybaby," because I'm a rain cloud.

That's horrible.

Thunder liked picking on me. When I cried, everyone laughed at me. I HATED being a rain cloud, so I ran away.

Poor Marshmallow!

We love you, Marshmallow.

I love you too. But I have to go home.

If you like it here, you could stay with us forever.

I can't bear to see everyone hurting because of me. The longer I stay, the worse the drought will get. I have to go home and fix everything.

Please stay just a little longer.

I won't be lonely, because I have all of you now.

Tell us if Thunder or any of the other stupid weather spirits give you a hard time.

Yes! Ping us in our dreams, so we can send them stink-bomb offerings.

You'll always be our team mascot.

It won't be the same without you cheering for us.

Even though we can't hang out like before, I'll cheer for you from up there.

Promise?

Pinky promise.

You may want to try another promise. Jordan's pinky promise is jinxed.

I blame Kemala for messing up my pinky promise.

How is it my fault? You used to swim like a sea slug.

Yeah? A sea slug who saved your butt a few times.

Marshmallow. Terima kasih for teaching our sea slug how to swim.

Take care,
Marshmallow.

AUTHOR'S NOTE

There are many stories about kids embarking on wild
adventures due to unexpected events. They get into mischief,
perhaps acquire magical powers, defeat monsters, fight
treacherous villains, and maybe even save the world.
Yet most of these children are able-bodied.

While writing this book, I did a lot of research into the
everyday life and sporting activities of paraplegic children
and athletes. I wanted to depict Jordan and her wheelchair use
with respect and accuracy. However, like any fantasy fiction,
I took creative liberties, giving our heroine a natural athletic
talent closer to a young Olympian's. While Jordan still
needs to work hard to learn a new sport, her learning
curve, stamina, and reflexes are above average.

Marshmallow & Jordan is a fantasy story set in Indonesia.
Jordan is a mortal girl with a physical disability, but she is
confident and determined. She does not let her use of a
wheelchair define her. She rescues a deity-in-training, survives
middle school, and achieves extraordinary success despite few
people believing in her. Marshmallow is her opposite. His image
is loosely inspired by Airavata, a Hindu white elephant
god who can knit clouds and helps Indra create rain. Marshmallow
inherits Airavata's supernatural power of controlling rainfall.
However, as a deity-in-training, he is insecure and timid.

Jordan gives Marshmallow unconditional friendship, while
Marshmallow broadens Jordan's horizons and helps her see
her potential. Though this is fantasy fiction, I hope that every
reader can see themselves in this story.

Visual development painting

Visual development painting

MARSHMALLOW'S MINI DICTIONARY

- Ayam goreng — Indonesian fried chicken

- Durian — A large tropical fruit with a strong odor and thorn-covered rind, which is considered the "King of Fruits" in Southeast Asia

- Ganesh — The Lord of Obstacles, the elephant-headed god, is one of the most worshipped Hindu deities.

- Halo — Indonesian for "Hello"

- Monyet Kecil — Jordan's dad affectionately teases Jordan, calling her "Monyet Kecil." *Monyet* means "Monkey." *Kecil* means "Little."

- Nenek — Indonesian for "Grandmother"

- Ojichan — Japanese for "Grandfather"

- Pisang goreng — Indonesian fried banana

- Terima kasih — Indonesian for "Thank you"

- Terima kasih banyak — Indonesian for "Thank you very much"

Marshmallow's Recommendation

Lemper ayam is a savory snack made of glutinous rice
filled with seasoned shredded chicken, wrapped in banana leaf.

Jordan's Recommendation

Onde-onde is a cute little traditional Southeast Asian
dessert made out of sweet glutinous rice with the center
filled with palm sugar. Nenek gives Jordan the nickname
"Onde Dikit" because onde-onde is Jordan's favorite
dessert. The funny way Jordan's family addresses her is
inspired by the quirky habit of nicknaming in my family.

Lynn's Recommendation

Jus alpukat is Lynn's favorite drink, and it's an authentic Indonesian smoothie. These sweet, rich, and popular avocado-chocolate beverages are made with avocado, milk, condensed milk, and chocolate. It's the perfect post-practice refresher.

Nenek's Recommendations

From left to right:

🌸 Sago gula melaka is a Malaysian pudding made from sago, pandan leaves, palm sugar syrup, and coconut milk. This version is wrapped in a banana leaf.

🌸 Bolu kukus is a soft and fluffy Indonesian sponge cake with a texture simliar to chiffon cake.

🌸 Jian dui are fried sesame balls made from glutinous rice flour with a red bean paste filling. This pastry originated in China back in the Tang Dynasty. Today, this snack is popular throughout Indonesia.

Visual development painting

MR. AL-SAMARRAI'S
FUN FACTS ABOUT INDONESIA

Borneo (Kalimantan)

Sulawesi

New Guinea (Papua and West Papua)

Sumatra

Java

Indonesia is a country in Southeast Asia and Oceania, between the Indian Ocean and Pacific Ocean. It consists of 17,508 islands, of which around 6,000 are inhabited.

The largest islands are Sumatra, Java, Borneo (divided with Brunei and Malaysia), Sulawesi, and New Guinea (divided with Papua New Guinea).

Indonesia is the world's largest island country and the fourteenth largest country by land area.

Indonesia lies along the equator. Its climate tends to be relatively even year-round: It's tropical with wet, hot, humid weather. However, the primary variable of Indonesia's climate is not temperature, but rainfall.

Instead of four seasons, Indonesia has just two: hot and dry, and the rainy monsoon.

Agriculture is a key component of the Indonesian economy. One of the world's largest agricultural nations, Indonesia exports a wide variety of tropical crops, including palm oil; natural rubber; cocoa; coffee; tea; cassava; rice; and tropical spices like pepper, nutmeg, vanilla, cinnamon, cloves, ginger, and cardamom.

However, in recent years, Indonesia has faced more severe drought than in the past. The harsh dry season makes the country more vulnerable to forest and peatland fires. The shifting climate significantly impacts the Indonesian Archipelago due to scarcity of clean drinking water and declining supply of irrigation water. This leads to crop failure.

Climate change is a global issue. Each of us can help reduce global warming by reducing our carbon footprint.

- ❀ Reduce, reuse, and recycle.
- ❀ Save electricity and water.
- ❀ Car rides are convenient, but walking or biking both save energy and are good exercise as well.
- ❀ Plant a tree or bee- and butterfly-friendly gardens.
- ❀ Be a science champion and raise awareness.

Small actions make BIG differences!

Visual development painting

Character design concept art

Acknowledgments

Thanks, Marietta, my amazing agent! Without her inspiration, this book would not exist at all! When I first wrote a story about a white elephant, it was a historical-fantasy picture book. Marietta suggested that I contemporize and expand the idea into a graphic novel! Marietta, your support and wisdom throughout this long creative journey has been invaluable.

Maria, I can't ask for a better editor than you, and I'm lucky you're also my good friend. Developing a graphic novel is a long, lonely process. I can't thank Maria enough for riding this "roller coaster" with me. Thank you for lifting me when I tripped and celebrating each milestone with me. You made this journey fun, even on days when we burned the midnight oil and worked in a hotel room on a holiday.

Anita! YES!! She IS the same Anita who owns Cold Whip Ice Cream in the book. But in real life, Anita is an art gallery owner. Anita and Maria were the first people with whom I shared the concept of *Marshmallow & Jordan*. Whenever I get exciting ideas or I freak out due to a work crisis, Anita generously offers her love or a shoulder to cry on and always cheers me up!

Last but not least: thank you, Calista, at First Second, for believing in my story and acquiring *Marshmallow & Jordan*.

🌸 Terima kasih, TEAM MARSHMALLOW!! 🌸

❧ To my Nenek, Mom, Dad, and Piglet. ❧

First Second

Published by First Second
First Second is an imprint of Roaring Brook Press,
a division of Holtzbrinck Publishing Holdings Limited Partnership
120 Broadway, New York, NY 10271
firstsecondbooks.com
mackids.com

Library of Congress Control Number: 2021906595

Our books may be purchased in bulk for promotional, educational, or business use.
Please contact your local bookseller or the Macmillan Corporate and Premium Sales Department
at (800) 221-7945 ext. 5442 or by email at MacmillanSpecialMarkets@macmillan.com.

FIRST

EDITION

First edition, 2021
Edited by Maria Ludwig and Steve Foxe
Cover design by Kirk Benshoff
Interior book design by Sunny Lee
Special thanks to Alex Blaszczuk and Jacquelyn Ryan

Sketched and cleaned up in Photoshop.
Hand-painted with watercolor on paper and digitally composited in Photoshop.

Printed in China by RR Donnelley Asia Printing Solutions Ltd., Dongguan City, Guangdong Province

ISBN 978-1-250-30061-4 (paperback)
1 3 5 7 9 10 8 6 4 2

ISBN 978-1-250-30060-7 (hardcover)
1 3 5 7 9 10 8 6 4 2

Don't miss your next favorite book from First Second!
For the latest updates go to firstsecondnewsletter.com and sign up for our enewsletter.